MW01119187

A Score to Settle

Journal by
Dante Burke

Published by
Murder Mystery Box

www.MurderMysteryBox.com
Caretaker@murdermysterybox.com

ISBN 9781091908826

Dedicated to the sleuths, the mystery solvers, the adventurers, members of the mysterious, and the seekers of intrigue.

Start of the Day

Today is the day. My hands won't quit quaking. I've had my job for a couple years. Never in that time has my mom ever paid me a visit at the park. She knows what I do and all, and to be honest, I never pegged her as one to come out and try it.

I work at Rickman Adventure Canopy Tours as a zipline guide. I've zipped hundreds of times. It's what I do every day, but I can't shake the stinking jitters today.

My mom and step dad are coming out for a tour and are bringing a few of their buddies from college along for the ride. I'm sure after the first few lines, I'll snap out of it.

It's a little odd to me. Not just that my mom wants to zipline. That's strange enough, seeing as she's afraid of heights, dislikes the great outdoors, and isn't much of a daredevil. The odd thing is, I've never heard her talk about these old college friends before. She knew my step dad from back then. Come to think of it, I don't recall Benton ever talking about his college friends either.

Benton has been my step dad since I was crawling. It was never a secret that he wasn't my biological father. My mother and Freddy, my biological father, dated in college. One day, he took off. My mom said that she thought the pressures of college got to him and he split. There was an investigation in to his disappearance, but in the end, they concluded that he must have ran off.

A few months after he left, my mom found out about me. She told me once, if he'd known about me, maybe he wouldn't have left. She would have known him about as good as anyone, I suppose. Benton and my mother became closer after Freddy disappeared. They were married when I was about six months old.

Benton's been here for me my whole life. Like I mentioned, neither one of them have talked much about their time in college. And they have never mentioned any of their friends from back then.

About a week ago, Benton received a strange call. I only think of it as strange because of his behavior. He covered the phone and started whispering. He took the phone to the garage and closed the door. After about ten minutes, he waved my mom to the garage. They stayed in there for about a half-hour. Then, they came out and acted like everything was normal. My parents have always been mostly open. I've never seen either one of them take a call out in the garage.

The next day they told me about some of their friends from college coming out for a reunion of sorts and that they'd be booking a tour at the zipline park. Here I am, a week later and they're all supposed to meet us at the park in a few hours. As strange as it is, I think it'll be interesting to meet some of the people my parents used to hang out with. Maybe some of them knew Freddy and can share a few stories about him.

It would be neat to hear a little more about him. He didn't have any close family for me to ever meet. All I know about him is what little my mom has shared with me. It's a sore spot for her. She doesn't like talking about him. My parents have provided well for me in a nurturing home. I've never felt the need to try to track down Freddy. He left his old life behind, that included my mom and me. It doesn't matter if he knew about me or not. He's never been a part of my life. He's a stranger to me. Nevertheless, it would be interesting to hear a few old stories.

I'll be recording the whole thing. That way, I can come back to my journal and write about the whole experience.

I need to get ready and head to the park. I have a tour of six that I need to guide before the whole *college reunion tour.*

Arrival

Almost everyone scheduled for my mom and step dad's reunion tour showed on time. I had Lana with me as the other guide. Lana is new here. She was only hired a week and a half ago. Typically, we have two guides per tour, but we've had three on our tours, during her training, up until yesterday. Lana's still in training, but she's passed the hand-holding phase of it. She did well on yesterday's tours and the one we had this morning.

She's had a couple complaints, but nothing that has stuck. For example, on her third day, a guest complained that she nudged them off a platform. Nobody saw it happen, so it became a he said, she said kind of thing. Another guest complained that Lana intentionally body checked him. Lana said it was an accident and no one else saw the incident, so it was simply noted in her file. Other than that, she's done well, so far.

Barb and her son, Lief arrived first. Lief is around my age. He went straight for Lana after they arrived. I couldn't hear what they were saying, as I aided Barb in putting on her harness. They giggled and whispered as Lana harnessed Lief. He wore baggy, cargo pants with about fifteen pockets. There was something odd about their interaction. It seemed like they knew each other.

"Barbara," A woman exclaimed. She approached with a man at her side. Barb squealed as the woman rushed to her. They hugged each other tightly, giving me the impression, it had been a while since their last visit.

"It's been a long time, Trudy," Barb said, eyeing the newcomers. "Have you and Graham been married all this time?"

"All this time," Trudy said with a grin.

"It's great to see you again," Barb stated. "I wish it were under different circumstances, but it's still a delight."

"It really has been too long since we've seen each other. Are you well? And what about your son?" Trudy inquired.

"Lief, come on over here and meet my friends, honey," Barb called out. She turned back to Trudy. "We're doing fine. We've had a few rough times lately, but nothing we can't handle. You know, teenagers..."

"I get it," Trudy nodded. "But isn't Lief an adult?"

"Of course, he is," Barb fidgeted. "You know kids these days. They don't want to leave the nest until they've got everything in order."

"Oh, so he's saving for a place of his own?" Trudy smiled, fluttering her eyes. "What does he do for a living? Is he in college?"

Barb's cheeks flushed. "He's taking a gap year while he decides on a major and is actively putting in applications for a job. How about you? Do you have children?"

"No," Trudy crinkled her nose. "Graham and I never had kids. You know me, I've never been the motherly type. In order to have kids, you've got to like kids."

"I'm Lief, Barb's son," Lief said as he approached.

"Good grief," Graham wiped his forehead. "You're a grown man. Sheesh! Time goes by so fast. I'm Graham, by the way. This is my wife, Trudy."

Graham looked to Barb and then to Trudy with wide eyes.

"It's nice to meet you," Lief said, shaking both their hands.

Trudy looked shaken in meeting Lief. I couldn't put my finger on it, but it looked as though Barb, Trudy, and Graham shared some sort of unspoken conversation.

Just then, my parents walked in.

"It looks like most of the old gang is here," Mom said.

"Stella!" Trudy called out, rushing toward Mom in the same fashion she'd approached Barb.

Trudy hugged Mom, then Benton. Graham followed his wife, hugging Mom and shaking Benton's hand. The four of them exchanged pleasantries, as I laid out the remainder of the harnesses.

Lief went back to Lana and chatted with her as she filled out the paperwork for the tour.

"Hey guys," a man called out as he arrived.

"Hans," Trudy smiled. She made her way to the new fella and hugged him like she'd done to all the rest.

After their embrace, Trudy and Hans strode toward the rest. I let them catch up for a few minutes, while I set up the last of the equipment.

Lana went around to all of them with her clipboard having them sign the liability release forms, Lief following her each step of the way. After all the forms were signed. Lana and I got everyone into their harnesses.

Because we have nine people on this tour, including Lana and me, everyone had a different color harness. We have ten different harness colors and can accommodate up to fourteen people per tour. I gave my mom, her favorite color, purple. Benton got blue. Lief's harness was gray and his mom's was pink. Trudy wore a red one and Graham ended up with an orange one. That left Hans in yellow, Lana in brown, and me in black.

Like I would wear any other color harness. Sorry, yellow's just not my color.

We gave each guest a paracord bracelet that matched their harness color. Lana and I also have a fifty-foot length of paracord attached to our harnesses. Lana has a predominantly blue toned cord and mine is green.

"Alright everyone, let's go over a few safety guidelines, then we'll start your ziplining canopy tour," I said.

"Wait," Trudy spoke out. "Faith isn't here yet."

"I tried calling her, but it goes straight to voicemail," Mom said.

"I see, she's on the list," I said. "She must be running behind. When she arrives, another guide can try to catch her up to us. In the meantime, we need to get going."

I went on to explain my opening spiel that I give to every tour about following directions and staying safe. Next, I had everyone follow Lana and me out to the ATVs. I loaded my parents, Trudy, and Graham into my vehicle. Barb, Lief, and Hans hopped into Lana's ATV and off we went.

I took the lead, heading up the three-quarters of a mile dirt road toward line one.

"Is everyone excited?" I asked.

"I'm stoked," Graham called back.

"Me too," Benton added.

"Have any of you zipped before?" I asked.

"Nope," Trudy said.

I looked in the rearview to see the rest shaking their heads.

"You're going to love it," I said. "Our longest line is seventeen hundred feet and our highest line is more than three hundred feet from the ground. You could reach speeds of up to fifty-five miles per hour."

"Are you trying to scare us out of this?" Mom asked with a chuckle.

"No way," I said. "You're going to have the time of your life. It's going to be a lot of fun."

I checked the rearview to see Trudy nudging Graham.

"Dead ringer," she said to him.

"I know, right?" Graham nodded.

"Who?" Mom asked.

"Barb's son," Trudy's eyes widened.

"Oh," Mom nodded.

I pulled my vehicle to a stop. Lana parked behind a few seconds later.

"Alright, folks," I said, hopping out. "That's as far as we go on wheels. It's all on foot from here. We have our first line coming up about fifty yards in. Let's get to it."

Open Evidence #1

Test Line

We hiked to the first line on our canopy tour. Lana and I escorted the group up the stairs to the test zip platform. I could see the nervous faces. Nearly all the first timers get the jitters on the test line. The test line is more like a practice line, the get the nerves out of the way and pump up the adrenaline.

This platform, like most of the others is rectangular in shape. It's all wood, with protective wooden railings that are four feet high. Under the zipline is a plank that extends out from the platform, blocked by a chain that clips into place. The protective wooden railings extend on both sides of the plank. Along the railings is a mounted, steel rail to clip in to for safety.

"Okay guys," I said. "First things, first. See this chain barrier? No one is to unclip this, under any circumstances. Every line has one of these chains. The only people that will touch this chain is Lana or myself.

"As you can see everyone has two clips hanging from their harness. One is attached to your trolley. This is what you'll use to zip across the line. It has handlebars you can hold onto when you zip. When it's your turn, take the free clip and clip it on to the plank railing. Once you're clipped in, one of us will open the safety chain and let you out onto the zip plank. This is for your safety. You must be clipped on the railing before you can walk the plank. Clipping onto the rail keeps you tethered.

"Once you're on the plank, we will take the trolley on your harness and clip it to the line. When the trolley is secured, we will unclip you from the rail and attach that clip to the backside of the trolley as well. Once you reach the other platform, we'll unclip you from the line and we'll be on to the next line. Everybody understand?"

I heard a few verbal confirmations and saw nearly everyone nodding. I clipped in and went through the chain and stood on the plank.

"This is our test line," I continued. "It's just to get us started. It's this line that will get us to line one. Line one is the first line with a view, we'll be zipping on. As the tour goes on, the lines will increase in length and in height.

"Our test line, here, is only fifty feet from the ground. As you can see, it's not that spectacular. It's over a somewhat plain, grassy field. But worry not, adventure seekers, the stunning views ahead on the other lines will take your breath away. Who wants to go first?"

"I'll go," Graham volunteered.

"Great," Lana said. "Have you ever ziplined before?"

"Sure haven't."

"You'll love it," Lana smiled. "First, I'm going to zip across to the other side. I'll show you how it's done. Once you zip across, I'll get you unclipped and everything."

"Sounds good enough for me," Graham said, wringing his hands.

Lana clipped in. I unclipped the safety chain for her to join me on the plank and reclipped the chain behind her. Next, I attached her trolley to the line, making a production of it for everyone to see. I unclipped her from the rail and connected her clip to the back end of the trolley.

Lana gripped the handlebars on the trolley for the benefit of the others. After glancing back to the tour group, she winked and stepped off the plank.

The group watched on as she zipped the line. Everyone wore a smile of some sort. Lief wore a smirk, while rubbing the back of his neck. Mom stared at the line, chewing her fingernails. A wide grin lit up Trudy's face as she tapped her foot.

Lana reached the platform and radioed back once she was safely clipped in and ready.

"We are a go, zip, go," Lana radioed.

Graham stepped forward, as I clipped him into the rail and removed the safety chain. I guided him out on the plank, clipping the safety chain behind him. Graham rubbed his hands over his pants and exhaled sharply, as I secured him to the line.

"Nervous?" I asked.

"Nah," he shook his head.

His wide eyes and shortness of breath told me otherwise, as did his white-knuckle grip on the rail. We get quite a few fellows that are terrified to zip, but would rather cut off their own hand than admit weakness.

"Zip away," I radioed to Lana.

"You are clear to go as soon as you're ready," I told Graham.

"Do I just jump?" He asked.

"All you do is step off the plank. You'll be to Lana on the other side in no time."

He took a deep breath and exhaled it in one big burst. He started nodding as if he were silently convincing himself that he could do it. I kept quiet, giving him the time he needed to draw up the courage to take his leap of faith.

"Yup," Graham whispered to himself. "Here we go. All righty, let's do this."

Graham waited a moment longer before stepping off the plank and zipping his way to Lana on the other platform.

Oohs and Ahhs were expressed by the others on my platform. Trudy squealed with delight and my mom clapped when Graham made it to the other side. My mom stepped forward pointing to herself.

"I'm next," she said in a high-pitched voice.

"Let's do this," I said.

I began the same clipping in and out routine as I always do, when I caught a bit of a conversation going on with the others. Benton, Trudy, and Hans were huddled in a group.

"Listen," Hans said. "Someone is on to us."

"Not now," Benton whispered. "We'll talk about this in a little bit. But not here and now."

"Finn and Maxie in the last week?" Hans said, reaching into his pocket. "It's not a coincidence. This note was taped to my car. Someone knows. They're coming for us."

Hans held up wadded paper.

"Let me see the note," Trudy said.

Hans passed whatever it was he pulled from his pocket to Trudy. After inspecting it, Trudy tossed the paper on the floor of the platform, not far from me.

"Nonsense," Trudy fumed. "It's ridiculous. This whole thing is being blown out of proportion."

"Go, zip, go," Lana called over the radio. It pulled my attention back to getting Mom across.

"Zip away," I radioed back.

"Okay, Mom you are all hooked up. Hold onto your handle if you want. Step off the plank and you'll zip across. It's a lot of fun. Trust me, when you reach the other side, you'll be eager to ride the next zipline."

Mom smiled, flashing her perfect teeth. She put her pinky in her mouth, biting at her nail. She spit out a nail clipping and huffed loudly. Her eyes sparkled as she grabbed her handle. She took three deep breaths and exhaled reminiscent of a woman practicing Lamaze. She glanced back at me and held her breath. With a shrug of her shoulders, she stepped off and zipped across to the other side.

"All right," I said. "Who's zipping next?"

Open Evidence #2

Line One

Everyone made it safely across the test line. Not that I had any doubts. The only one I suspected might not go through was Hans. He hesitated a couple of minutes. Eventually, he stepped off the plank like everyone else.

For line one, I went across first, and Lana stayed behind to send the guests to me. One by one, nearly all of them had zipped across without incident. Usually, once they zip the test line, the initial jitters fade away. The guests know what it feels like and trust that the line is safe. It opens them up to enjoy the remainder of the lines and take in the scenery and beauty surrounding them.

Line one zips over a canopy of trees with birds swooping over and through the treetops. The fresh wind presses against your face as you feel the sensation of flying above the forest, like an honorary bird.

Almost everyone had zipped across line one. I was still waiting on Lief and Benton. No surprise that Lief was one of the last ones left. I think he's got a thing for Lana. The thing is, I'm fairly sure Lana has a boyfriend. Lately, she's hinted about spending time with a guy.

"Go, zip, go," I called.

"Look," I whispered, pointing to the mountainside. "Wild turkeys. They're about twenty yards out."

The guests hurried to the side of the platform glimpsing at the bobbling birds scampering deeper into the forest.

"That was neat," Barb gasped. "Too bad Lief missed it."

"He'll get his chance," I said. "Maybe not turkeys, but I'm sure he'll see some wildlife out here."

"Zip away," Lana radioed.

I turned away from the guests on my platform waiting for Benton or Lief to zip my way.

"Listen," I heard Hans whispering. "I am freaking out here, man. Did you guys get a note?"

"You need to calm down," Graham said.

"Calm down, huh?" Hans huffed. "First, Maxie dies in a tragic scooter accident. Then not even a week later, Finn dies in a horrific accident. Now, where's Faith? She never made it. I talked to her last night. She was all set to be here. She's dead too. I just know it. These aren't accidents. Someone is after us."

Benton came across the zipline a little on the fast side, but I caught him. He was all smiles as he clutched me into a hug.

"This is really a lot of fun," he laughed.

"Glad you like it, Dad," I smiled.

It's cool that my parents are ziplining with me. I love what I do. It's exciting to share it with them. I can see from their faces that they're enjoying themselves.

"Look at this flower," Barb expressed. "Does anyone have a knife I can cut it with?"

"Here you go," Graham said, handing Barb a pocket knife. "Hang onto it 'till the end of the session. I'll get it back at base camp."

Barb nodded in agreement and proceeded to use the all-gold knife to cut a small bushel of white flowers from a low hanging tree branch. She tucked the flowers in her harness.

"It's obvious that either someone knows or it's one of us," Graham whispered to the others.

"One of us?" Mom said.

"No one, but us, knows about what happened," Trudy pointed out. "It's only logical to think that one of us is behind this. Whatever this is."

"Isn't it possible that Finn and Maxie's deaths were actually accidents?" Barb asked. "Bad things happen, you know. It could be a simple coincidence that we're all getting bent out of shape over."

Hans threw his hands up. He sighed and circled. "Where's Faith, then?"

"There are a thousand reasons why she might not have made it," Trudy growled.

"Yeah," Hans crowed. "One of them being another accident."

I turned my attention back to the zipline. Lief and Lana are the only ones left on the other platform. Whatever is going on with my parents and their old college buddies sounds serious. I don't want to be nosey, but I can't help but overhear their conversations.

It sounds like they were involved in something a long time ago. Whatever it was, might be coming back to haunt them. I don't want to inject myself into their business, but I'm feeling a little concerned for my parents' safety, if Hans is right. There have been two deaths in their circle of friends, possibly accidents, possibly not, and another person who didn't make it here today. I see why Hans is concerned. I don't know what kind of trouble they're in, but I'm getting worried.

"Go, zip, go," I called on the radio to Lana.

"I'm afraid that I need to side with Hans on this," Graham lowered his voice to a whisper. "There are coincidences in the world, sure. That doesn't explain the note. What we did… There's no denying that whatever is happening right now is because of what we did."

"Al was a monster," Trudy said softly. "He deserved what happened. The way he harassed Maxie and Hans was despicable. Hans had to drop out of college because of Al. He lured in Barb, a naïve young girl, bedded her, dropped her, and ruined her reputation. He wronged us all. Let's not forget that. So, if one of you is having a crisis of the conscience, you need to knock it off. We are the only ones who know about what happened. It can only be one of us."

"Is it possible that it is Al that's doing this?" Barb asked.

"It's not Al," Benton lowered his voice.

I cleared my throat and tapped my boot. Where is Lief? Why hasn't Lana sent him yet.

"Go, zip, go," I called once more.

"Zip away," Lana called back.

I don't know what the stinking hold up could have been. Obviously, the others don't think I can overhear their conversations. I don't know why they chose the zipline park to hash out whatever it is that is going on between them. I thought they were simply getting together to catch up on each other's lives. They should have met in a more private setting. I don't want to be involved in any kind of drama, especially my parents' drama.

Line Two

Lief and Lana safely zipped across line one.

The guests seemed to be enjoying their time so far on the tour. Lana and I pointed out some of the beauty in the nature around us.

"We have some Swamp Hickory trees over here," I explained. "And that over there, is a White Oak. They can live up to 450 years and grow to be upwards of a hundred feet."

Lana cleared her throat. "White-tailed deer are all over this area. Keep your eyes out and you'll likely spot one or two. At dusk, they come out in the masses. We also have a few black bears in this area as well as coyotes. No need to be alarmed, they rarely are spotted, and we have no record of them interacting with anyone in this area."

"This next line," I added. "Zips across Canyon River. Be sure to take in the stunning views from this line."

Barb pulled the knife from the pocket of her skin-tight jeans and searched for another place to put it.

"You want me to hang onto that for you?" Lana asked.

"That would be wonderful," Barb smiled. "It's digging into my leg."

"No worries," Lana laughed. "Just let me know when you need it."

Lana strode to the plank and crossed the line first. I started sending the guests her way.

I felt grateful that I didn't overhear the guests continue their previous conversation. Instead, they expressed their excitement for this line and how exhilarating ziplining had turned out to be.

It didn't take long for everybody to make it across the line to the next platform. Everything went smoothly, which is exactly the way I like it. I zipped the line last, taking in the view of the river and forest while practically flying. Once I made it across, I was faced with a confused expression on my mom's face.

Mom looked around and she grinned at me.

"Have we hit a dead end?" She asked.

The platform we stood on did not lead to another zipline. It looked similar to the other platform, except only one zipline was attached and that was the one we all zipped in on. I smiled and strolled to a pulley system located on the opposite end of the platform.

"Our canopy tour is meant to expand your sense of adventure. We hope that you will push the boundaries of your comfort zone in an effort to show you that you are only limited by you. We are going to rappel down from this platform. We'll hook you up and all you have to do is let go of your fears."

"Oh, my goodness," Barb mouthed.

Lief rubbed her shoulders and smiled. "It'll be all right, Mom."

"Let's do this," Benton nodded.

"I like your enthusiasm," Lana giggled. "I'll go first and then you all can rappel down to me. It's thirty-feet down, but Dante and me do this every day. So, you're in good hands."

With that, Lana clipped her trolley into the pulley and rappelled down. The pulley system only allows for a few feet at a time to pass through the trolley before it applies the brakes. Then it releases for another few feet and so forth until the guest reaches the ground.

Everyone watched over the railing as Lana made her way slowly to the ground. Benton went first. He rappelled down as if he'd done this before. Lief went next. One by one they all took their turns making it to the safety of the forest floor.

"How did that feel?" I asked, after reaching the ground.

"Invigorating!" Graham hooted.

"Fantastic," I said. "We are going to take a quick pit stop, here. We have some berries and nuts that are local to the region set up at a serving station over there."

I pointed to a concaved table made from a hollowed-out tree.

"We also have an outhouse," Lana added. "Just in case. It's twenty yards out that way."

Benton patted my mom on the shoulder and widened his eyes. "I'll be back in a jiff."

He headed out in the direction of the outhouse. Trudy, Barb, and Hans followed. I led my mom, Lief, and Graham to the food station. Lana strode up the path toward the next line to ensure that the path is free of any debris or any trip hazards.

"Here we have spring onions," I said. "We also have blackberries and walnuts. These all grow wild in the area. Go ahead and try some."

We bring along a bag of these regional snacks on every tour. Since Lana is the rookie, it's her job to bring them along and set them out. After rappelling down to the ground, she went to the station and laid out the snack items before anyone else made their way down.

The guests tasted the snacks, chatted amongst themselves, and explored the forest. Since this is a part of the tour, this area of the forest is moderately clear from the foot traffic. We generally take a break for about ten minutes or so in this area before moving on to the next line.

It wasn't long before nearly everyone was intermingling with each other. Lief stood near the snack station. My mom and Barb had spotted birds fluttering around a nearby shrub. Graham, Trudy, and Hans were not far from me taking up a conversation on a previously discussed topic.

"Benton was Al's best friend," Trudy whispered. "We all know what he did to Benton. Any woman Benton took a liking to, Al swooped in and stole her from under his nose. Al thought he was God's gift to women. As soon as Benton showed interest in Faith, Al took those terribly embarrassing photos of her. When Benton showed interest in Barb, well, we know what happened there."

"Okay," Graham hushed his voice. "We get it. He was awful to Benton. He was awful to us all. The real question is, who is doing this, and does it have anything to do with Finn and Maxie's accidental deaths?"

Lana emerged from the path. With a nod, she conveyed that we are ready to move forward to the next line.

"Okay, everyone," I called out. "We are ready to get going to the next line."

"Where's Benton?" Mom asked.

I scanned the area. Benton was not in sight. In fact, I don't recall seeing him try the snacks or exploring the area. The last time I saw him was almost fifteen minutes ago. It's not like him to go wandering off alone.

"When's the last time anybody saw him?" I asked.

"He used the outhouse first," Trudy said.

"Yeah," Barb added. "He was heading back this way. I'm surprised we made it back before him."

"Maybe he's exploring a different path," Trudy mentioned.

"Okay," I sighed. "Lana stay here with the guests. I'll be right back."

I made my way through the forest toward the outhouse. The forest is in full bloom this time of year, which camouflages much of the area. I could hear my mom and the others calling out for Benton as I jogged up to the outhouse. I gave it a knock and checked inside, but no Benton. I called out to him a couple times. There was no response. Where could he have gone? I searched the area, but didn't find any trails that he might have followed. It was like he disappeared.

With the forest shrubbery and trees so full and thick in this area, it's nearly impossible to tell if he went charging through the forest. I shook my head. This forest is wrought with thorn bushes and spiky vines, making it an unappealing place to take a hike. Not to mention that Benton isn't the type to do something like that.

After calling out for him several more times, I decided to rejoin the others to see if he'd turned up. I jogged back to them only to find that he was still missing. I shook my head.

"I couldn't find him. He's not answering when I call out," I sighed.

"What's this?" Lana asked.

It was some sort of paper tacked to a tree.

Open Evidence #3

Line Three

We've been searching for Benton for nearly a half hour and we've turned up nothing. This has never happened before. We've never lost a guest in the forest. Plus, Benton is my step dad, I know him. He would never leave us here to worry like this.

My mom has been back and forth between crying, calming herself down, calling out for Benton, and then back to crying. We need to get help out here to find Benton. As the lead guide out here, I need to control the situation. I have to keep my cool and keep everybody calm.

"Everyone," I shouted, waving the others over. "Gather around over here."

I stood near Hans and Graham. Lief, Lana, and Barb approached us from behind. Trudy draped her arm over my mom's shoulder and gently, guided her toward us.

"I need everyone to remain calm," I said. "I'm sure Benton went wandering off into the woods and got turned around. We need to get back to base camp to get help in finding him. From here the only way to get back is to keep following the course."

"We can't leave Benton," Mom snarled.

"Can't we radio for help?" Hans asked.

"I'm afraid we are too far from base camp to get a signal," Lana added.

"Did anyone bring their cell phone?" Graham asked.

"No, we all locked them in the lockers before we left," Barb shrugged.

"Even if someone brought their cell, there's no service out here," Lana said with a sigh.

"I'm not going anywhere," Mom confirmed.

"Listen," I said. "Benton is a strong and resourceful man. If he's fallen or injured, he'll know what to do to stay safe. We need more assistance out here to find him. We've been looking for him for too long. We need to get reinforcements out here to find him and get him any help he may need. The longer we stand around and argue about it, the longer until he's found. If we hurry through the lines, we could likely make it back in an hour."

"Why don't you zip back and bring help out to us?" Mom asked.

"I can't do that," I said. "It's against regulations and it's unsafe. At least two guides must be present while the ziplines are in use. We all need to stay together. Come on, follow Lana."

Lana began the trek to line three. Everyone except my mom and Trudy followed as directed.

Mom came up to me and pulled me into a mama bear hug. She sobbed on my shoulder. I hate it when my mom cries. I could barely hold it together during that hug. I knew I needed to stay strong for everyone out here, but especially for my mom.

"Let me stay behind," she pleaded.

"I can't, Mom. If something happened to you out here, not only would I be responsible for it, but I couldn't live with myself knowing that I could have kept you safe. We will find him. I promise. For now, we have to go so we can get help to find him."

Mom nodded and walked along the path with Trudy ahead of me.

Though I tried to project confidence and control, internally, I felt a wreck. It's one thing for Benton to have gone off the trail and got turned around. That doesn't account for him not answering our calls out to him. Sound carries well out here. Voices and sounds echo off the trees. He should have heard us. My best guess is that he fell and knocked himself out. Otherwise, why wouldn't he have answered us?

Then, there's the note on the tree. It seems like someone's playing a trick. Could Benton be involved somehow? I hope not. If this is some sort of prank that my parents and their friends are trying to play on me or on each other, I'm going to lose it. Nothing about this is funny.

It didn't take long for us to reach the line three platform. We climbed the stairs to the platform which took us about thirty feet from the ground. This line zipped above the tree canopy and across the mountain. We typically highlight the height of this line at 270 feet and the 1200-foot length of this line to the guests, but with Benton not with us, it didn't feel right to play up the next line.

With a nod to me, Lana clipped in and zipped across to the other side. While she zipped, everyone on the platform remained silent. I'm not sure that anybody knew what to say at this point.

"Go, zip, go," Lana radioed.

"Mom," I waved her to the plank.

She stepped forward with a devastated expression on her face. I clipped her in the rail and removed the safety chain. When she was out on the plank, I reclipped the chain.

"Zip away," I called back to Lana.

"It's going to be okay, Mom. We'll find him."

"I love you, Dante. I love you so much."

"I love you too, Mom. You can go whenever you're ready. The quicker we move through the tour, the quicker we can find him."

She took a moment to wipe the tears from her cheeks. With a deep breath, she stepped off the plank and zipped across.

I could hardly contain my frustration. I wanted to punch something. Clenching my jaw, I turned back to the others to find Lief behind me.

"I'll go next," he said.

"Sure," I said clipping him in. "You, uh, got a thing for Lana?"

Lief grinned. "Yeah, I guess you can say that."

"I don't want to ruffle your feathers, but she's got a boyfriend."

"Is that so?" He smiled, stepping out on the plank. "You know anything about this boyfriend of hers?"

"I know she's got one and that's enough for me," I said.

"Go, zip, go," Lana called.

"Zip away," I called back, clipping Lief's trolley to the line.

"Whenever you're ready," I told Lief.

"What if I told you that I'm her boyfriend?" Lief chuckled and stepped off the plank, zipping the line.

Lief doesn't talk much, but he's a little on the strange side.

I turned back to see Barb ready to go next. I wasted little time getting her all set to get across the line.

This day has turned out to be stinking bizarre. I can't wait to make it back to base camp, find Benton and be done with all this. This group of people my parents brought out here bring too much drama.

"Who do you think left the note?" Trudy asked in a whisper from behind me.

"Could it be Benton?" Hans asked.

"Don't be ridiculous," Graham said. "Benton wouldn't do something like that. It has to be someone else that knows."

"No one knows except us," Trudy urged.

"It could be Al," Hans suggested.

"It's not Al for crying out loud," Trudy growled. "It has to be one of us. Right now, my best guess is Benton. Or Faith. Maybe she made it out here after all. Maybe she couldn't live with what happened anymore and snapped. Someone is doing this and if we don't figure it out soon, we could end up like Finn and Maxie."

"This is our punishment," Hans whispered. "We are going to get what we deserve."

"Don't forget what Al did to all of us," Graham said. "He nearly ruined me and Trudy's relationship in college. He tried to seduce her and when she refused him, he started those nasty rumors. Trudy was jumped and put in the hospital because of those rumors.

"And how about the photos of Finn and Faith? He followed them back to her house and spied on them from outside her bedroom window. He took those topless photos of her and distributed them all over the school, mailed them to her parents, and slipped them into the pews at church. Al got what was coming to him."

I cracked my neck. I don't know what these people are talking about, but it sounds like some serious stuff happened back then. I took a deep breath. Lana radioed the go ahead, not a moment too soon.

"Whenever you're ready," I said to Barb. I then turned to my radio, "Zip away."

Without hesitation, Barb zipped along to the next platform. Next up was Hans, followed by Trudy, then Graham. I zipped across to find the guests in a commotion of sorts.

"What's going on?" I asked.

"There's another note," Lana informed me. "Stella found it when she zipped across."

"Mom, where did you find the note?" I asked.

"It was pinned to the rail by the next zipline. That's not all, this article was with it."

Something is going on, here. It's about time that my mom and all these other people start coughing up some answers.

Open Evidence #4

Line Four

After reading the note and the article, I felt my blood boil. Something is going on, here. Whether it's some elaborate prank or something much darker, it needs to stop. As it is, Benton's whereabouts were unknown, something that has never happened on a tour before.

I zipped across first, leaving specific instructions with Lana to send my mom first. As I zipped across, I glanced down at the trees below. It's an amazing view. About three-quarters of the way across the line there is a stream below with a tiny waterfall. No matter how many times I zip this course, I never get tired of the views. This line ends on a deck elevated only a few feet off the ground. From this line, we walk about twenty yards to the next platform.

I felt like I was waiting on the deck for ages, before Mom came zipping my way. After detaching her from the line, I waited to radio Lana for the next guest.

"Mom," I said in a stern tone. "You have to tell me what's going on."

"I'm not a hundred percent sure," she shook her head.

"Then, tell me what you do know."

"I'm not sure where to begin. It's a long story that spans back decades."

"No one else is zipping across the line until I have some answers," I shook my head.

"It's about your biological father," Mom rubbed her forehead.

"My father? Freddy?"

"Yes. Freddy is what I called him. His real name was Alfred."

"Is this the Al that everyone has been talking about?"

"You heard?" My mom asked, pacing the deck.

"Of course, I heard. You are having these conversations only a few feet away from me. What did you guys do to him? And who's leaving these notes?"

Mom paced the deck some more, looking everywhere except at me.

"I don't know who's leaving the notes and I'm not sure why."

I heard a brief burst of static come from my radio.

"Hey, what's going on over there?" Lana called over the radio.

I took a deep breath. I glanced at my mother. She looked exhausted. I wasn't getting anywhere with her. The others involved in all this should be here for the rest of the conversation.

"Go, zip, go," I radioed back.

One by one they all zipped line four and landed safely on the deck. Once Lana unclipped her trolley from the line, I turned back to the others.

"Somebody here needs to give me some answers," I said, addressing my parents' college friends.

I carefully looked over each one of them. Suddenly, they were tight lipped. This entire tour they have been whispering and chatting about past secrets and current threats, but now, they haven't anything to say. With my stepfather missing, finding threatening notes, and my own birth announcement pinned to a tree, I want answers. And these people have a few answers to give.

"I agree with Dante," Leif said with a nod. "You guys have been whispering around like your selling state secrets. We've found these threatening notes and we have a member of our group missing. One of you has got to know what's going on, if not all of you. So, spill it."

"Leif, honey," Barb began. "You need not worry about that, honey. We just need to get back to base camp. That's the most important thing and that is all you need to worry about."

"Is someone here playing some sort of prank?" I asked.

"Oh, no," Hans rolled his eyes. "This is all very much real. There is no joke going on here. Two of our friends from college have died in accidents in the last week. The thing is,

I don't think they were accidents. I think they were killed on purpose and the killer made their deaths look like accidents."

"Oh, you have got to be kidding me," Leif gasped. "Why on earth would someone kill two of your friends in a week and make it look like accidents? Does this have anything to do with this Al person, you guys keep talking about?"

My mom exchanged glares with Trudy, Graham, Hans, and Barb. None of them said a word. It was as if they were trying to tell each other to keep it zipped using eye contact alone. If that's what they were trying to do, it worked because none of them said a thing.

As much as I want answers and to get to the bottom of what's going on, I'm starting to lose patience. We need to get through the rest of the lines and get back to base camp where we can call for help for Benton. Whatever else that's going on here between my parents' former college buddies, they can sort out amongst themselves some other time.

"Is anyone going to answer me?" Leif bobbed his head to the side. "I want answers. No, I demand answers."

"Leif, honey," Barb approached, patting her son on the shoulder. "We'll talk about this later. You don't need to worry about any of this."

"I'll give you an answer," Hans muttered. "Someone killed our friends and they are coming after us next."

"Hans!" Graham shouted. "Are you kidding me? Keep your mouth shut. These people don't need to know our business."

"These people?" Leif tilted his head. "I'm Barb's son, so if my mom is in danger, then it's my business. This guy right here, Dante, is the son of Stella and Benton. And let's not forget, Benton is currently missing. I think it goes without saying that whatever's happening is definitely his business too."

"I'm not doing this anymore," Graham threw his hands up. "I need a second to myself, if you don't mind."

"Don't go too far," Trudy instructed.

I started after him only to find Trudy standing in my way.

"Let him go," she said. "He won't go far. It's all flat terrain here. He needs a minute or two to clear his head."

With that, Graham stormed off into the forest. He disappeared into the shrubbery after a few seconds. I didn't want him walking off on his own. We all know what happened to Benton, well, strike that, we have no idea what happened to him. Even though I didn't like the idea of him all on his own, perhaps it was better to let him calm down. The last thing we need is for someone to lose their cool and swing on someone else. At this point, it feels like the only thing missing from this tour… is a fist fight.

"We shouldn't have met here," Mom said, chewing her nail.

"It was Barb's idea," Hans shrugged. "She wouldn't take no for an answer."

"What does it matter where we met?" Barb probed. "The scenery doesn't matter. It's the personalities of certain people that cause drama."

"Excuse me? Is that a jab at Graham?" Trudy growled. "Why was it so important to meet at the zipline place?"

"It wasn't even—" Barb began.

"Let's keep things calm," Hans said. "We don't need to talk about this now, when everyone is so high strung."

We waited several minutes for Graham to come back. Everyone had pretty much kept quiet as we waited for him to return. I looked at my watch, he'd been gone for about fifteen minutes.

Trudy noticed me checking my watch. She half shrugged and bit the inside of her cheek.

"Graham," Trudy called out. "We need to get going, Graham."

We waited for him to emerge from the forest or to call back. Graham didn't call back, and he didn't come out of the forest, either. Trudy called out to him three more times. All yielded the same results.

"We need to look for him," Lana mentioned.

I shook my head, not in disagreement, in disappointment. I knew he shouldn't have gone off alone. That's why I tried to go after him, but instead of controlling the situation like I'm supposed to do, I let Trudy talk me out of it.

"Lana and Hans," I said. "You're with me. We'll go out and look for him. The rest of you stay here on the deck until we return. Do not leave the deck for any reason until we get back. If Graham makes it back before us, then give us a shout."

The others nodded in agreement.

Lana and Hans followed as I led the way into the forest. This tour is growing more unbelievable by the minute. Where the heck did Graham take off to? He doesn't know his way around out in the forest. I hope he doesn't think he can hike back to base camp from here. It'd take a full day's hike from this spot on the mountain.

I'm going to have a lot of explaining to do when we get back. I am the lead guide. Not only has my step dad gone missing, but now another member of the group has disappeared. I cannot go back without Graham. My job is about to be toast.

To think, the very first time my parents come out for a canopy tour and all hell breaks loose.

“We need to split up to cover more ground,” Lana suggested.

“Not going to happen,” I huffed. “There’s no way we can lose another person out here.”

“I have a radio,” Lana added, rolling her eyes.

As much as I didn’t want to admit it, she was right. The forest is too thick in this area. It’ll take hours for us to search these woods. It could take hours, even if we split up.

“Okay,” I said. “Take Hans with you and stay together. Keep in radio contact and we’ll keep each other posted on our positions.”

“You got it,” Lana said, waving Hans to her. “We’ll check downhill and you check uphill?”

“Sure,” I nodded.

My chest felt shallow. I didn’t like this idea, but what other choice do we have.

This part of the forest is on a slope. I watched Lana and Hans make their way downward. After a few seconds of hesitation, I began my trek up the slope. I heard Lana and Hans call out for Graham. I waited a few minutes before doing the same.

I’d searched the forest for about twenty minutes before Lana called over the radio and checked in. Her search had yielded the same results of mine, nothing. I crisscrossed my area, calling out for Graham from time to time, but I never received an answer.

I spent another ten minutes searching, finding no sign of Graham or that he'd even come this way.

"Graham!" A feminine voice sounded in the distance.

I reached for my radio. That voice didn't sound like Lana. Last time She checked in with me, she was too far from my position for her voice to sound so clear.

"Lana, your position?" I called on the radio.

"I'm about fifty yards southeast of my last position," she called back.

She's nowhere near me. Whose voice did I hear?

"Who's out there?" I shouted.

"Dante? Is that you?" The voice answered.

I hurried through the woods toward the sound of the voice.

"Yes, who's out there?" I shouted.

"It's Barb. Where are you?" She called out.

"Stay where you are. I'll be right there."

My mind raced as I kept going in the direction of where I'd heard her voice. Why is Barb way out here? I told them to stay on the deck. Are the others with her? If Barb is out here, surely Trudy is out looking for her husband.

It only took me two minutes or so to reach Barb. I felt relieved to find her. It seems that all day I've lost people, it felt a little triumphant to finally find someone I was looking for. The only problem was that Barb was alone. I expected to see Trudy with her.

"Why are you out here?" I asked.

"I'm trying to find Graham," Barb said, matter-of-factly.

"Did everyone else stay on the deck like I instructed?"

"No," Barb planted her hands on her hips. "We waited and waited, but nobody came back. Trudy wouldn't wait any longer. So, we decided we should all look to save time."

"Even my mom?"

"Yeah," Barb shrugged.

I sighed, shaking my head. I can't believe the stinking people in this tour. I just can't... I really can't believe that none of these people can take instruction. Worst of all are my parents. First, Benton goes off on his own and who knows what happened to him. My best hope is that he somehow got turned around and is wandering around. Who knows?

Now, everyone is all over this forest. I have to go around and corral everyone up and get them back to line five. I still don't know where Graham is or if anyone has found him. In all my time working here, I've never lost a single person in the forest or had so many people undermined my instructions.

I just want to scream at everyone. I wish there was some way to get them all back to base without having to finish out the remaining lines. This is going to cost me this job. I know it is.

A scream echoed through the forest. The scream sounded south of my position.

"Lana," I called on the radio.

"Barb, come with me," I said, heading down the mountainside.

"It wasn't me," Lana called back. "It's not far from me. Head down to my last location, but further east. By the way, I have your mom and Lief with me. I guess they all came out looking for Graham."

"Okay," I called back. "I've got Barb. We're coming toward you."

Another scream sounded south of our position. It was followed by shouting. I couldn't make out the words, but the yelling continued as Barb and I made our way down the mountain.

As we approached where the screaming had originated, I could hear more shouting. Again, I couldn't make out the words, but I could hear that there were multiple voices involved. I pushed past stray tree branches, wild shrubbery, stepped over fallen logs and large rocks, all with Barb on my heels.

We came upon the group at last. Lana, Hans, and Lief stood off by a few yards. Trudy sobbed, while on her knees. My mom stood behind Trudy, rubbing her shoulders. I wasn't sure what was going on, but at least they were all here. All except for Graham. Back to square one.

"What's going on?" I asked in a stern tone.

"Something has happened to Graham," Trudy croaked between sobs. "This is his boot."

I looked at the scene before me. I wasn't sure what was going on, but I did know that we needed to keep moving. We can't stay here in the woods. And, we definitely can't keep searching for Graham. We need to get to safety and get help out here.

"Trudy," I said, approaching her and pulling her to her feet. "Drop the boot and nobody touch anything."

Open Evidence #5

Line Five

We need to get back to base camp as soon as possible. I know that this fiasco is far from over, but the first step is to get everyone back to base camp. There are three lines left for us to zip to make it back. Once we make it to line seven, I can radio base camp to let them know what's going on. Base can get help out to line two and line four to search for Benton and Graham.

It took a few minutes to calm Trudy's hysterics. She didn't want to leave without Graham. Luckily, my mom stepped in and explained that she is equally concerned for Benton, but that getting back to base camp is the best option in finding the missing men. After some convincing, we got Trudy on board.

Lana and I led the guests about twenty yards east of the deck where we landed on the last zipline. The platform stood at the edge of a cliff and the zipline hung far above the treetops.

Line five is our longest line at nearly seventeen hundred feet. It's about three hundred feet off the ground, at midpoint. It's an exhilarating line, far above the forest. I think it's as close as it gets, to feeling what it would be like, to be a bird soaring above the trees. Ordinarily, I would build this line up to the guests, but not today. We need to get through this course as quickly as possible.

We climbed the stairs to the platform. I zipped across first this time. One by one, everyone followed until Lana made it across last. It felt reassuring for everything to go as planned. One more line and I can radio for help. Two more lines and we'll be back to camp.

I've been in guide mode all this time. Now that we are so close to getting back. It's hitting me hard that Benton is missing. I am trying to think positive about his situation. That's all I can do. I'm worried, though. He's been here for me my entire life. I can't imagine things without him.

For most of my life, I've known that he was my step dad, and that's how I've always spoken of him. In truth, he's the only father that I've ever known. He's the one who's raised me and taught me about life. I wish I'd referred to him as my dad all this time and not as my step dad.

"What's this?" Lana asked. "Oh wow, it's another note."

The others huddled around the landing ledge where we'd all zipped into. Not another note. I didn't want to go see the stinking thing. It didn't matter what was written on the note. I'm tired of these games. I still wasn't sure if this was some sort of prank that one of them was playing or if something nefarious was in the works. I simply wanted to make it back to base camp and put all this in someone else's hands.

Lana took the note and passed it to me. I grabbed it and shoved it into my pocket.

"I don't know what all this nonsense is," I said. "But we need to keep moving. We're almost to camp."

"I disagree," Lief huffed, waving his hand to the side. "I want answers. What are these notes all about? I mean they are here for a reason. What does Alfred have to do with anything? Why are these notes here? Obviously, they have something to do with you all."

"I want some answers too," Lana chimed in. "Are we all in danger? If so, I want to know why."

I sighed. Of course, I want to know what this is all about, but more importantly, I want to get back to base camp. We can get our answers then. I don't understand why we need to make a big deal about it now.

"Honey, we can talk about this later," Barb whispered, reaching for Lief's hand.

Lief pulled his arm away sharply. "Did you guys do something to Alfred?"

Barb's mouth gaped. She cocked her head to the side, wordless.

"Nobody did anything to Alfred," Trudy murmured. "He was a terrible person that tormented just about everyone who entered his orbit. He ran away, probably out of guilt. He took off for whatever reasons and started a new life somewhere. Obviously, he doesn't want to be found."

"I don't buy it," Lana shrugged. "You all knew Alfred. Then, you get together and magically, these notes start popping up on our tour, this is not a coincidence. Could this Alfred person be out here, enacting his own revenge on you?"

"No, he can't," Hans stated.

"How can you be sure? According to you and the articles, he disappeared?" Lief asked. "Why couldn't he be back to bother all of you?"

Hans rubbed his hand over his forehead and his cheeks, before wiping the back of his neck. He glanced at Trudy with cold eyes, then to my mom with a hard blink. Shaking his head, he glared at Trudy. She shook her head at him.

"I think someone here is doing this," Hans uttered. "I think that someone here is deranged. Someone here, has come unhinged. I wish I could say I knew who it was, but I don't."

"Why would one of us do any of this?" Lief asked. "And what does it have to do with Alfred? I want answers, Mom."

Barb took a deep breath and glanced at the others. Her eyes grew watery as she looked to the sky.

"Honey," Barb whispered. "I need to tell you something. Back when I was in college, I fell for Alfred. Not to get too detailed, he was my first. He used me to get what he wanted and then he dropped me like I was nothing. Not long after, I found out I was pregnant with you."

"Wait," Lief protested. "Are you saying?”

"Alfred was your father," Barb confessed. "He wanted nothing to do with you or me. He acted like we were trash, blowing in the wind. That's the kind of person Alfred was. So, I said that to you because you deserve to know the truth. Alfred died a long, time ago—"

"Barb!" Trudy shouted.

Trudy charged forward to Barb and put her hand over Barb's mouth. In doing so, Trudy fell into her. Barb took a step back and shoved Trudy off her.

"Not another word," Trudy shouted.

"Don't you—" Barb started. She stumbled backward toward the plank for the next line.

Thankfully, the safety chain barrier was in place, but it didn't stop me from holding my breath.

Barb fell against the chain barrier. It was as if it all happened in slow motion. I could feel myself leaping forward toward Barb, but I felt like my body was twice as heavy and slow as usual. Barb hit the chain, back-first. I reached for her outstretched arms but couldn't get there in time. The chain broke open on impact. Barb's face shriveled up like a raisin. Her eyes squinted nearly closed and her lips pressed tightly together as she fell from the platform. It was an expression that will haunt my nightmares for years to come. Barb fell from the platform to the forest floor below.

I immediately tied off to the platform and rappelled down to Barb. It goes against policy, but I couldn't not go down and help her. She looked like she was sleeping on the vines beneath her. There was nothing gruesome about the scene. Her body rested on the ground as if she'd simply fainted. I checked for vitals.

Barb was gone. There was no life left in her.

I attempted CPR, but I knew she wouldn't be waking up. Still, I tried. I don't know how long I worked on her, as far as time goes, but I kept going until my arms were sore. All the while, I tried my hardest to block out the crying and sobs coming from the platform above me.

The others looked over the railing of the platform down at me. I shook my head.

"I'm sorry," I uttered, looking to Lief.

He fell to his knees and began wailing. Lana bent near and rubbed his back. My mom and Trudy embraced, and Hans stood nearby, shaking his head.

I looked away.

I can't understand any of this. How can everything go so wrong? It's like anything bad that could happen, has happened.

I glanced back up at the platform. My eyes drifted to the safety chain dangling off the plank. I looked twice. Something caught my eye.

Open Evidence #6

Line five (still)

I climbed back to the top of the platform. My eyes met Lana's. Her eyes widened and her lips pulled to a side smirk. We are the only ones here that didn't know Barb before today. I feel responsible. I am the lead guide and it's my job to keep everyone safe. We've had a fatality. Plus, there are two more missing guests. Forget my job. I'll be lucky if I make it out of all this without getting arrested.

I examined the clip on the end of the safety chain. It's not our clip. We don't use these janky clips. The clip on the chain is like a keychain carabiner. No wonder the chain didn't hold. Why was this clip here? Where is the one that's usually there? How did the clip get switched out?

It's one thing if there is some sort of old college drama between my parents and their friends. This is taking it to another level. This is no practical joke. What's happening is real. Barb is dead. *She died.* The thought crossed my mind that Benton and Graham could be playing some hide and find me game, but after all this, there's no way. Someone changed that clip.

Trudy tried calming Lief, but he was adamant about going down to his mother. Mom aided in trying to soothe Lief's grief. He sat on the platform floor with tears falling from his cheeks. Every few seconds, he'd wipe his tears with his inner wrists.

I held up the small, keychain clip.

"Who wants to talk to me about this?" I demanded.

All eyes were on me. Their expressions told me they didn't know what I was talking about.

"Who replaced the real carabiner," I held up the one on my harness. "With this clip?"

I raised the small clip again.

"What are you talking about?" Lana asked, crossing the platform to examine the replacement clip. "Where did you get this?"

"I took it from the broken safety chain. It was this clip that gave out when Barb fell into it. If the proper clip was there, it would have caught her."

"How did that happen?" Lana gasped.

"That's what I want to know," I said. "Who is sabotaging us? Who swapped the clips?"

My mom, Trudy, and Hans looked at each other. Lief was still on the platform floor, sobbing. I didn't want to rub salt in his wounds, since he'd just lost his mother, but I wanted answers. Someone did this and I want to know who.

"I don't know anything about all this ziplining stuff," Trudy said, bobbing her head from side to side. "Only the instructions you gave us. I haven't been paying attention to the clips and ropes. I just hang onto my handle when I go on the line and that's it."

"Son," Mom said. "I don't know anything either."

"I only got across the line," Lana muttered. "A few minutes before she fell. I don't know anything about it, Dante. I know better than to do anything like that and put someone's life in danger. Could one of the other teams have done it during their last tour?"

"Why would they do that?" I asked, raising an eyebrow.

"I don't know," Lana shrugged. "Maybe they lost or dropped the real carabiner and needed something to secure the chain and slapped on that small clip for now. Then they forgot to put the right one back on."

"That's pretty farfetched," I said. "And dangerous. If one of the other teams did that, then they are responsible for what happened to Barb.

I looked to Hans and waved him to the side, away from the others. In light of all this drama from their days in college and things regarding Alfred, Hans has seemed more forthcoming than my parents and the rest of their friends.

"You need to tell me what's going on," I said.

Hans nodded, "It's all coming back to haunt us."

He rubbed his hands through his hair and wiped his upper lip.

"What are you hiding?" I asked.

Hans licked his front teeth through closed lips. He glanced at Trudy and my mom.

"We did something," Hans sighed. "Everyone who came today and two others. Their names were Maxie and Finn. A long time ago. Alfred was a guy who tormented us back when we were in college. He picked on and bullied some of us and used some others. He ruined college for some of us and changed the course of our lives in other cases.

"Things all came to a head one day when we were at the river. We were all out there, when he showed up with Kristen Holt. Alfred was up to his usual antics. His behavior disturbed Kristen enough that she left. Benton thought about leaving too. He should have left...

"Graham and Alfred got into it. Maxie joined in and was screaming at Alfred. Things were getting out of hand. Benton rushed over to help the situation, but only made it worse."

From across the zipline platform, Trudy cleared her throat. She shot a bitter glare at Hans. Folding her arms, she stormed our way.

"What are you talking about Hans?" She huffed.

"I'm telling Dante what we did," Hans admitted.

"I think not," Trudy scowled.

"We've kept this a secret for too long. We need to come clean. Look at what's happening," Hans threw his hands in the air.

"He is delusional," Trudy said, looking to me. "He suffers from paranoia. I'm serious. He's on medication and everything. Isn't that right Hans?"

I turned back and looked at my mom. The truth is what I need, and she can give it to me. All Mom needs to do is come over here and straighten things out.

Mom bit at her fingernail. She peeked at me with grieving eyes, then she turned away.

I sighed. My mind is all twisted right now. No one wants to be straight up because they are hiding something. Lies. They all have lies that they're hiding. Just how important are keeping these lies a secret? To what lengths are they willing to go to keep quiet?

"You killed him," I said, looking at Trudy and Hans.

"No, we did not!" Trudy crowed.

"It was an accident," Hans placed his hand on his chin. "It was an accident, at first."

"Hans!" Trudy shouted.

"Stop!" I yelled back at Trudy. "Just stop. Keep quiet and let me talk to him."

Trudy gasped and took two steps back. Her expression twisted to that of disgust. I didn't care if I offended her. I want the truth and she is butting in and preventing me from getting it.

"What happened?" I asked.

Hans took a deep breath, "Alfred hit Maxie in the face. Benton lost it and punched Alfred a couple times. Then, Graham tackled Alfred to the ground. They fought on the ground for a few seconds. They were both caked in mud by the time we separated them. Alfred elbowed me in the ribs and got loose. Finn and Barb tried to stop him, but he knocked both down. He knew full well Barb was pregnant at the time and he still threw her to the ground.

"Alfred was almost to Benton, when Faith tripped him. He went sliding through the mud. Finn and I grabbed Alfred and held him on the ground. Then, Graham and Stella joined us in restraining him. We got him to his feet. He struggled the whole time. Mud flung all over the place. We pulled back on him, but he slipped out of our grips. He fell and cracked his head on a rock. There was blood everywhere.

"We didn't know what to do. We freaked out. Some of us worried about going to jail or being kicked out of college. We were kids. Stupid, stupid kids. Trudy and Benton took him out in the water to make it look like he'd hit his head and fell in the water. Then, he woke up. Alfred started struggling in the water. He realized what we were doing to him and tried drowning Trudy. Maxie and Stella swam out to them. The four of them worked together to hold Alfred underwater until he drowned."

I covered my mouth with my hand. My parents have been keeping this secret my whole life. I can't believe my parents and their friends killed my biological father and kept the secret all these years.

Who *are* these people? I feel like I don't even know my parents at all. How could they do something like this? And keep quiet about it for two decades?

"What did you do with him after that?" I asked.

"We let him float down the river like the log that he was," Trudy said.

"Why is this all coming out here and now?" I asked.

"I don't know," Hans said. "Finn and Maxie recently died in what looks like tragic accidents. That's why we decided to get together to figure out what is happening."

I strode to my mom, but she wouldn't make eye contact with me. I tilted my head to the side, hoping for something. Anything.

"I have nothing to say about this," Mom said firmly, chewing on her fingernail.

"We deserve answers," Lief shouted, in a croaky voice. "No matter what a jerk Alfred was, he was still our father."

I understand that Lief's going through a lot, with the revelation that Alfred was his father and with the death of his mother. But it seems like Lief was speaking just to be heard. Neither, he nor I, knew Alfred in any capacity.

"We need to keep moving," I said.

"I am not leaving without my mom," Lief cried.

"We can't bring her, Lief," Lana said. "The sooner we get back to base camp, the sooner we can send someone for her."

"I'm not leaving her," Lief insisted. "Lower me down, so I can be with her."

"It's not a good idea," I said. "Lana's right, we need to get going. We'll send help for her."

"No!" Lief shouted. "She is my mother and I'm not going anywhere without her. I'm not leaving her here all alone. I'm not doing it."

I took a deep breath and scratched under my eye. I don't know how this day could get any worse. It has to be the worst day of my life on so many levels. I am not a real emotional guy, but today is testing me. I feel wiped out. I'm exhausted. I don't even have the time and space to let everything sink in. I am still responsible for the rest of the people here.

"Fine," I sighed. I wiped my brow and waved Lief over. "I'll lower you to your mom. You need to stay with her and not go anywhere until help arrives, okay?"

Lief nodded, wiping tears from his cheeks.

"You're really going to let me stay with her?" He asked, waving his hand toward the plank.

"Yes, but you need to stay right here."

"Why are you letting me stay?" Lief asked, leaning in. "I mean, don't get me wrong, I'm not leaving her here, but why aren't you trying to make me keep going like you did with your mom and with Trudy?"

It was a good question, but not a hard one.

"Benton and Graham are missing," I said. "They are likely lost in the woods. If that was my mom down there, no one would be able to get me to leave her."

"Thank you, Dante," Lief pursed his lips.

Before I realized what was going on, Lief wrapped his arms around me. He hugged me tight. I was so shocked, I didn't know what to do with my hands.

"Lana," I said, gently pulling out of the embrace. "Give Lief your radio so we can keep in contact with him."

Lana nodded. She clipped the radio on Lief's harness.

I tied my paracord to a clip and attached it to Lief's harness. For leverage, I wrapped the cord around my body to lower him to the ground. I tied off the loose end of the paracord to the platform railing. Lief sat in his harness as I lowered him to his mother, below. I untangled my cord from my body and left it tied to the platform.

"I should be able to radio for help at the next platform," I called down to Lief. "Twenty minutes, tops, before they should get here to get you and your mom."

Lief gave me the thumbs up as he crouched over his mother.

I took a deep breath and got the chills. I couldn't imagine what I would've done if it had been my mom down there.

Line Six

Ordinarily, Lana and I would talk about the indigenous trees and the stunning view that this line afforded, but in the face of what we've been through so far, it's just not happening. Plus, my concern for Benton is growing. I've got a bad feeling. I'm really worried. My stomach feels hollowed out thinking about him. I've done my best in trying to avoid panicking, but I feel nervous.

Once across line six, there is a seventy-foot rope bridge that connects the line six landing ledge to the line seven, ground-level deck. We clip into an independent cable that is a few inches above the rope bridge. We follow the bridge to our final line, which is a deck at ground level. Then, we'll zip line seven, landing on another ground level deck, fifty yards from base camp.

I clipped in and zipped across line six. I tried to let my worries melt away, if only for a minute or two. For a few moments I felt free of all that has happened. The wind pressed against my face, almost making my eyes water. My arms were outstretched to my sides, fighting the opposing force of the air.

Once I reached the platform, I radioed to base camp, but the response was garbled. I glanced at the rope bridge from line six to line seven. I'm sure I should come in clearly once

I cross the bridge. First things first, I need to get everyone across line six.

Since I had Lana leave her radio with Lief, I told her to send the guests to me in two-minute intervals, prior to my zipping the line. I checked my watch, in about twenty seconds, she'll send the first guest.

As I waited, I tried to figure out this mess we're all in. Could Alfred have survived? Is he back to seek revenge for what these people did all those years ago to him? If so, why did he wait so long? Why hasn't anyone else seen or heard from him all these years? What is so special about now? There has to be something I'm missing. If it's one of my parents' college pals, why did they wait until now to raise all this chaos?

I noticed my mom zipping the line toward me. She zoomed in with a somewhat excited look on her face.

"Oh, that was incredible," she said, breathless.

I smirked, not in a happy way. It was more of, *in annoyance.*

"Dante," she whispered. "I know you want answers, but now is not the time."

"People are dying, Mom. When is the time? After I'm dead?"

"You aren't in any danger," she shook her head, picking at her fingernail.

"How is that?"

"Whoever is doing this is targeting the people involved with what happened to Alfred. You weren't there." "How is it that you are so sure that I couldn't be collateral damage?" I asked. "And what about you? What am I supposed to do if something happens to you? Did you see what happened to Barb? How about how hurt Lief is? Dad is missing. We have no idea what happened to him. If now isn't the time, then the time may never come."

She shrugged. "I understand your frustration. I do. I cannot speak about this. Not right now and not with you. I'm sorry, but I can't."

I clenched my jaw and exhaled through my nostrils. Shaking my head, I turned away from her and back to the landing ledge. With a quick check of my watch, I figured, my next guest would be zipping in soon.

I turned back to my mom. She stood there looking smaller than I'd ever seen her before. I don't know if it was her posture, or if it was how disappointed I was in her, that made her look that way to me.

"Mom, you can clip into that cable and go across the rope bridge, whenever you're ready," I said, pointing to the cable.

She nodded and clipped into the cable as directed and began making her way across. Ordinarily, I think she would have waited, but I think with the tension between us, she wanted to distance herself from me.

Soon Trudy was on her way in. She had a similar expression on her face of exhilaration after riding line six. I instructed her to cross the bridge.

It only took a few minutes for Hans and Lana to make it my way, as well. I had them go ahead of me across the bridge.

The rope bridge is a V-shaped, suspension bridge made entirely of knotted rope. The knots are close enough on the sides that nobody can fall out, even if they weren't clipped in. The knots at the bottom of the bridge are tight enough that not even a foot can pass through.

I crossed the bridge rather quickly. I go across this bridge multiple times per day. The bridge ends at the line seven deck.

I tried radioing base camp, again.

"Base camp, base camp, this is team Dante. Comeback," I called.

I waited a few seconds, glancing to the others. I realized something was off but couldn't put my finger on it.

"Go ahead, team Dante," Jackson, from the front office, responded.

A wave of relief washed over me in hearing his voice over the radio. All this time, I've felt like we've been on our own.

To hear back from base camp made me feel a hundred pounds lighter.

"Base camp, we have big time troubles. I have two guests in the wind and one casualty," I radioed.

"Say again. You have a casualty? And two missing guests?" Jackson's voice spiked.

"Affirmative," I called back.

"Where are you? And confirm the number of guests with you," Jackson demanded.

"I am on the deck for line seven with Lana. We have three—I" I stopped short, releasing the radio button.

I glanced around at the others. Where is…

"Does anyone know where Trudy is?" I asked.

The others looked to each other, shaking their heads.

"She was just right here," Mom shrugged.

"Trudy!" I shouted.

The rest of the group began calling out for her, but there was no answer.

Not again…

"You cut out," Jackson radioed. "How many guests do you have at line seven?"

I sighed and popped my knuckles.

"Two guests," I whispered into the radio.

"Hold on a second," Jackson called. "The paperwork says you started out with seven guests. If you have two missing and one casualty, how do you have two left?"

"I started out with seven, yes. One went missing at the break station after line two. Another went missing at line four. We had a casualty on the line six platform. The victim's son opted to stay behind with her. He couldn't be persuaded otherwise. And now, on the line seven deck, another one has gone missing. I think someone is out here taking these guests."

"You think someone is abducting the guests from your tour?" Jackson murmured.

"Yes," I said. "The police and paramedics need to be called right now."

"Sure, yeah, okay," Jackson responded. "I'm calling now. Get the remainder of your tour back to base camp asap."

"Will do, over," I called back.

I began searching the area looking for Trudy. Without me directing the others on what to do, they all followed me around the forest in search for our most recent missing guest. What is happening?

"Trudy," Hans called out.

There was no answer.

"Where did she go?" I asked.

"She was right here with us," Mom said.

I shook my head and continued to search. I saw no signs that anyone had come this way in the forest. Disappointedly, I turned back. I needed to get the remainder of our tour back to base camp. We don't have time to keep looking.

We hiked back toward the deck for line seven. The last line of the canopy tour. After that, a fifty-yard hike and we'll be back to base. I hurried my pace in anticipation of getting this whole thing over with before someone else goes missing, or worse.

A scream echoed from behind me. I turned to see my mom with her hand cupped over her mouth. She stared at something in the shrubbery. Lana's eyes welled up and her skin paled as she clasped my mom's shoulder. Hans turned away.

I hurried to where they stood. There in the bushes, I found Trudy. She was face down on the ground between a shrub and a Shagbark Hickory.

"I can't believe this," my mom whispered.

"I tried to tell you," Hans said, behind gritted teeth. "I tried to tell you all, but nobody would listen to me. And now, we're almost all dead. I told you."

I knelt close to Trudy and slightly shook her shoulder. She didn't react. With a deep breath, I turned her over. On her neck, there was a reddish blistering from ear to ear. On the ground beneath her was the rope used in the attack. Someone strangled her from behind. I checked for a pulse, knowing full well I wouldn't find one.

I placed her back in the way I'd found her. I looked to the others with mistrust. I didn't trust any of them, even my mom.

"What's that?" Lana asked, pointing to the ground beside me.

The killer, once again, has left something more for us to find.

Open Evidence #7

Line Seven

I gathered everyone to the deck for line seven. We all were shaken after finding Trudy. I think we all felt more of a sense of danger at this point. After all, Trudy was right there and somehow, she was taken, lured, or wandered into the woods to meet the stinking person behind all this.

"I'll go ahead first," Lana volunteered.

"Nah," I said. "I'll go."

"I think you should stay to make sure everyone makes it on the line," Lana insisted.

I tilted my head. "You don't think you can handle that?"

"Yeah, of course I can. Fine. You go."

It struck me then, that Lana was frightened. She wanted this tour to end just as badly as I did. And it makes sense that she wouldn't want to hang back and be the last to zip across. Trudy was killed a few yards from here.

"No," I said. "You go ahead. I'll zip last."

"Are you sure?" Lana asked eagerly.

"Yeah, go on. The sooner you zip the sooner we all can. We'll be done with all this in a few minutes. I'll send them two minutes apart, like last time."

Lana needed no further cues. She quickly clipped her trolley in and away she went.

Line seven isn't the highest or the longest line. It's a fun enough line that zips through the trees and relatively close to the ground. If you looked at the canopy tour like a workout, the test line would be the warm up and line seven would be the cool down, but with a better view.

The landing for this line is another deck at ground level. Then, it's only a small hike along a well-worn trail back to base camp.

I took a moment to myself after I sent my mom & Hans across the line. Piecing all the information and things I've seen and heard today proved to be overwhelming. I'm worried about my dad. I have a bad feeling that he might not be lost in the woods.

My hands began to tremble, and I couldn't catch my breath. I had to push the thought from my mind, otherwise, I couldn't zip this last line. I suddenly had a thought, or rather, a suspicion. I reached for my radio, my hand shaking all the while.

"Switch to emergency channel and stand by," I called into the radio.

I switched my radio to channel nine, which is our designated emergency channel and waited for a response.

"Rodger. Standing by," Jackson radioed back.

I clipped in and zipped the last line on the tour. When I reached the landing ledge everyone was in a tizzy. They were all shouting at each other.

"It has to be you!" My mom shouted at Hans.

"If it was me, why would I have called everyone here?" Hans yelled back. "I think it's you! You happen to be right beside everyone who's died. Because let's face it, I'm pretty sure they're all dead."

"Calm down!" Lana yelled.

"Me?" Mom squealed, scowling at Hans. "I could never. But *you* are a nutcase. A medicated, whack-job. What happened? Did you go off your meds or something?"

"Whoa! Whoa!" I said, stepping between them. "What is going on?"

"There's another note," Lana said, pointing to a tree near the deck. "And something else."

Open Evidence #8

After looking over what was left for us to find. I think I know what's going on. While, I wouldn't be so bold as to say I know everything that's happened out here, I would say that I think I know who's behind all this.

I never thought the day would turn out this way. Having my parents come out to the park, seemed like a dream. I thought we'd all have an adventure and they could see what I do every day. Now, I feel like I know way too much about their secrets and lies.

I wish this day never happened. Oh, how freaking great it would be to wake up and find out this was all a stinking dream.

As much as I'd like to forget about all this, I need answers. I need to know what happened to my Dad, and to Graham.

Note from The Caretaker

Pardon the Interruption.

It appears that this is where Dante thinks he's uncovered the truth behind the deaths and disappearances during their zipline tour at Rickman Adventure Canopy Tours.

If you have been following along and reviewing the clues, this would be the part in this adventure that you make your attempt at solving the case.

Based on Dante's journal entries and the clues he gathered, do you have a prediction of who is responsible and why? If you do, then read on to the conclusion. If you do not, you can take time to review the evidence and journal entries before proceeding.

Please note, that the solution to this case shall be revealed in the next section.

We all stood on the landing deck after zipping line seven. Emotions were still running hot, but I'd slightly calmed the situation. While everyone seemed more than ready to hike back to base, I needed a couple more minutes with these guests.

I depressed my radio button and kept my thumb on it.

"We all need to have a discussion before we head to base camp."

"Now?" Hans asked. "We're almost to base."

"Yeah," I sighed. "We need to have it now, before something happens to someone else."

My mom put her hands on her hips and shook her head. She began pacing the platform as she bit at her nails.

"Something to say, Mom?"

"There's nothing for us to talk about," she puffed. "Hans is right. We're so close."

"Except someone killed Trudy. That means we're all in danger and we don't know who we can trust," I closed my eyes.

"Dante, we should go," Lana insisted.

I turned to my trainee. Although my blood boiled with anger and frustration about this entire situation and all the lies swirling around it, I knew I needed to keep my cool.

"How long have you known Lief?"

"What?" Lana took a step back.

I waited for an answer. The question didn't need repeating. She heard what I asked.

"Did you know Lief before today?" Hans asked.

Lana shook her head slightly and backed away. Her eyes shifted between us. After a moment, she closed her eyes for a long blink.

"Me and Lief," she took a long exhale through her nose. "We've been seeing each other for a few months."

"Why did you pretend you just met?" Mom asked.

"We didn't pretend anything," Lana snapped. "We didn't mention it, and no one asked, so…"

"Why didn't Barb know who you were?" Hans asked.

"I've never met her. Lief said that she was overbearing and critical of anyone he dated. He said she'd chase me away. Why are you asking me this? What does it matter if I was seeing Lief?"

I paced. Looking down at the ground below. My body rumbled as I tried to think of what to say next.

"Lief is behind all this." I said, looking to Mom and Hans. "He's the one who's been playing all these games and who's responsible for Barb and Trudy. I don't know what he's done to Graham and Dad, but I think the outlook for them is grim."

"Dante," Mom gasped. "How could you say a thing like that? He's just a young man. He's around the same age as you. There's no way a boy like that could have done all this."

"You might be underestimating the guy," Hans said, turning from Mom to me. "Why do you suspect Lief?"

"At first, I thought it was one of you," I nodded. "I thought somebody in your old college clique was pranking the others. I figured you guys must have bullied some guy named Al back then and were trying to get a rise out of the others.

"Then, as things began to unfold, I realized the secrets were much deeper and darker than I could have imagined. Mom, you made sure that I knew that Benton wasn't my biological father. You sold me the company line that you've been selling for decades. You told me, my dad's name was Freddy and that he took off before he even knew you were pregnant with me.

"I've always been happy with you and Benton and took what you said as the gospel. I never felt any need to look into or inquire about my bio-dad, once I got older. I felt happy in my life and never thought it was worth my time to look for someone that didn't want to be found."

"How does this prove Lief did any of this and why would he do it?" Hans asked.

"That's what I'm getting to," I said. "Lief didn't grow up the way that I did. I'm pretty sure he tried to look into who his father was, and from all that has happened, I think he found out. Alfred was Lief's father too."

I looked to my mom and Hans. They exchanged glances. Mom picked at her thumb nail. Hans pulled at his harness and exhaled out his nostrils.

"Barb never told him," I said. "I think Lief found out about who his father was and dug into Alfred's disappearance. Lief figured out what you'd all done and arranged all this to enact his own brand of justice."

"Lief didn't do anything," Lana growled. "This is all just your wild imagination. Everything you've said is all a complete guess out of left field. How dare you accuse him, especially when he's not here to defend himself?"

"You're right," I said. "It is a guess, but not a wild one. I've pieced the information together from what's been said and what I've witnessed. And yes, I am accusing Lief, but he is here. He can come out and defend himself at any time."

"What do you mean?" Mom asked.

"He killed Trudy," I said. "He didn't stay with Barb like he said he would. He's out here in the forest."

Mom peered over her shoulder. Hans scanned the trees and shrubbery around us.

Lana laughed, "Do you know how paranoid you sound? Who's to say it isn't you doing all this? Alfred is your father too. Maybe you're looking for justice for your *real dad.*"

"First off," I said. "Benton is my *real dad.* He is the one who raised me. And he did a great job. Other than my mom mentioning Freddy to me a few times when I was growing up, I never took interest in finding out anything else. Why would I have any reason to doubt what she'd told me?"

"I hate to play devil's advocate," Hans began. "But I have to agree with Lana, where's the proof to any of this?"

"Let's start with Trudy," I said. "The cord that was used to kill her was mine."

"Ha!" Lana shouted. "You are the killer."

"I left my paracord behind with Lief," I explained. "I tied it off to the platform, to lower him down to Barb, before we zipped the next line. The only way my cord could've been used to murder Trudy, is if Lief brought it there."

Hans gasped.

"The thing is, Lief was not alone in this plot to find his own brand of justice," I said. "You were in on it too, Lana."

"You're nuts," Lana laughed.

"Way back, when we found Graham's boot," I explained. "I found a little piece of your harness on the ground. I thought it strange, but I didn't quite put it together at the time. I was still in the mindset that this was all a prank. I think there must have been a struggle with Graham, and that's how a piece of your harness ripped off.

"It wasn't until we found the last note that I put things together. The knife pinned to the last note belonged to Graham. He lent it to Barb. Then, Barb gave it to you. Once I saw the knife and I recalled how you wanted to go first across the line, I knew you were a part of all this."

A rustling from a nearby shrub caught my attention. We all turned our gaze to the disturbance. Lief emerged with a smirk on his face.

"So, you think you've got it all figured out, huh?" He blustered.

"What did you do with my dad and Graham?"

Lief chuckled, curling his upper lip into a snarl.

"They got what they deserved," Lief gloated. "I'll just say they won't be home for dinner tonight, or any night and we'll leave it at that."

Mom fell to her knees. She buried her face in her hands.

In the back of my mind, I'd had a feeling that Dad wasn't coming back to us. I didn't want to face it. I wanted to believe that he'd be okay, that he'd simply got turned around in the forest. A tear snuck down my cheek, as I tried to stay strong. My chest felt warm like I'd taken a shot of whiskey.

"We are brothers," Lief began. "They killed our father… and got away with it. It's only fair that I return the favor. I found out about Alfred a few months ago. My mom had me clear out the attic and I found some of her old diaries. She never mentioned specifically what happened to Alfred, but she did write that he was my father. I dug up all the old articles. Tracked down everyone on social media. I figured it all out. Then, I made a plan. The police suspected them but couldn't prove it."

Hans shook his head, "How did you think you would get away with this?"

"The same way you did," Lief said. "My brother, here, will vouch for me, won't you, Dante? We're in this together. We're family. They killed our father. I'll take care of Hans and Stella. All you need to do is stick with the story that Hans felt guilty and he did all this."

"What?" Hans shouted. "First, you're not putting this on me. Second, you think you can take care of me? You've got to be joking."

"Graham and Benton were a lot bigger and stronger than you," Lief said. "Besides, I have a gun. You've got to have an end game."

Lief pulled a gun, from a side pocket of his cargo pants, and held it out by his side.

"Wait," I said. "I have a few questions."

"I thought you knew it all," Lana added.

"Why are you involved in this?" I turned to Lana.

"I love Lief," she began. "We have a deep connection to each other. What's important to him is important to me. Besides, I know what it's like to grow up without a father. His mom and her friends robbed Lief of a life without his father. They deserve to pay for their sins."

I shook my head. Who would think that this girl has such a drone-like mindset, that she'd do anything for love? Even murder? According to Lana, they've only been seeing each other for a few months. Some people… Some people are just stinking nuts.

"How did you set all this up?" I asked, turning my glare to Lief.

"First," Lief smirked. "I needed a way to get everyone together. I sent Lana out here to get a job with you. It was always my plan for this to go down at the zipline park. Next, I slipped the note to Hans in the mail knowing it would get to him in a few days. Finn and Maxie were my first two kills. I set them up to look like accidents. That way, no one would come looking for me.

"I followed Maxie on her scooter for a few days. Once I learned her route, I ran her off the road. It was a lot easier than I thought it would be.

"With Finn, I watched him for a while, too. He liked his gin. After he passed out on the couch, I slipped in and removed the batteries from his smoke detectors. He was out cold, didn't move an inch. I started the fire in his bedroom with a candle beside the bed. All I needed to do was drape his blanket over the candle and it looked like he forgot about a lit candle before he passed out, drunk.

"From Hans' social media platforms, I could tell he was the most insecure. That's why I sent him the note. It worked perfectly. When he got it, he looked everyone up and found that Finn and Maxie had just died. That sent his paranoia into overdrive.

"He contacted the others. I listened in on my mom's conversations. Once I realized that they were planning on all getting together, I urged my mom to let me tag along. She wasn't on board at first, but eventually she caved. I always get my own way with her. Originally, they were all going to meet at TinTown amusement park. I convinced my mom to get everyone on board with ziplining. That way, Lana could be here and you, Dante."

"It all came together even better than I expected. First, I took care of Faith this morning. I found her number in my mom's phone and asked her to meet me before the tour. I told her it was about Alfred. That got her attention. It was all so easy…I'll just say, she's a goner in the trunk of her rental car at the Binty Café parking lot. Then, once we got on with the tour, we lured Benton into the forest and put him out of his misery. Graham, that was perfect. Him, taking off into the forest like that, well, the opportunity presented itself like a gift wrapped present. When I stumbled upon him, he admitted to hearing us call for him, but he was too stubborn to answer.

"My mom was another one that just fell into our laps. Lana swapped out the clips. I was actually going to *bump* into Trudy so that she would fall. Before we could even put our plan into motion, Trudy flipped out and sent my mom over the edge.

"I'll admit, that one was a little sad for me. I knew my mom had to pay for what she'd done. And, I had every intention of punishing her, but that one snuck up on me a little bit."

"You're sick!" My mom screamed. "She was your mother!"

"I may be," Lief smiled. "But, my mom stole my father from me. You all did. You murdered him and covered it up. He never got the justice he deserves. Time to settle the score.

"Time's up. I need an answer, Dante. Are you with me? Cause these two need to be handled. You, me, and Lana can walk out of here just fine or you can go down with Stella and Hans. It's up to you. You don't need to die today."

I eyed some motion in the forest to my right. I let out a heavy sigh and released my thumb off the radio button.

"I think there's an alternative to all that," I said. "Everything you said was being broadcast from my radio to base camp. You aren't going to hurt anyone else and you're not getting away with what you've done.

The sounds of movement in the forest grew louder, before several people emerged from behind trees and shrubbery. It was the police. They approached with their guns drawn.

Lief put his gun down and the police arrested him and Lana without protest.

It's been a few weeks since Lief and Lana unleashed their reign of terror in the zip park. Lief and Lana are awaiting the start of their trial. Despite admitting to what they'd done in the zip park, they still pled not guilty. I'm not looking forward to seeing either one of them again when I have to testify, but I have to do what's right.

My mom and I are still adjusting to things without Dad. We had his funeral a day after Graham's. The police had found their bodies in the woods. Graham had been struck in the head with a rock and then tossed down the mountainside. Benton had been stabbed with Graham's knife and hidden in shrubbery. Trace amounts of Dad's blood was still on the knife when police tested the blade.

Faith had been found by authorities exactly where Lief had said he left her. They allege that she was suffocated in her vehicle by Lief and placed in the trunk of her car.

Life is different, now. It seems like the world has lost a little of its light, to me. I'm taking it day by day and doing my best to enjoy whatever time I have left on this planet. It's taught me that we never know which day will be our last. All we can do is make the best of the time we have.

Case Closed

Made in USA - Kendallville, IN
1156747_9781091908826
02.15.2021 1654